Nursery

ILLUSTRATED BY JESS STOCKHAM

Time to get up! Let's get dressed!

My feet are ticklish! Where's my t-shirt?

What's for breakfast? This tastes good!

Eat up, quickly! Would you like fruit?

Have a great day. See you later.

Look! There's my friend. Shall we run?

I like the cat sticker. Is this my peg?

I can't reach. Who needs some help?

Peep-o! What are you painting?

This feels squishy. Roll it out flat.

Oh no! I've spilt it! Watch out!

I like this crown. Can I be a nurse?

Join in everyone! I'll tap the tambourine.

Clap your hands and stamp your feet!

I love cheese. What's in your snack box?

I'm really thirsty. Do you like juice?

Quiet, everyone! Now, listen carefully.

I wonder what will happen next?

Catch! Throw it back to me.

Next on the slide? Let's make sandcastles!

This trike is fast.   Can I go in the car?

These seeds are tiny. What are you planting?

Look at my painting! Can I come tomorrow?